P

O ——————— O

H

Bee
Tree

Scones
and rox

My House

Eeyore

First American Edition. Copyright © 1999 Disney Enterprises, Inc.
Based on the Pooh stories by A.A. Milne
(copyright the Pooh Properties Trust)
All rights reserved under international copyright conventions.
Published in the United States by Grolier Enterprises Inc., Danbury,
Connecticut. Grolier Books is a division of Grolier Enterprises, Inc.
Originally published in Denmark by Egmont Gruppen, Copenhagen.
ISBN: 0-7172-8908-7
Manufactured in the United States of America.
A B C D   1 2 3 4

Disney's

Winnie the Pooh
&
The Honey Tree

GROLIER
BOOKS

One morning, deep in the Hundred-Acre Wood, a little bear named Winnie the Pooh was doing his stoutness exercises.

"Up, down…up, down…up, down…"

Pooh felt a rumbly in his tumbly. Exercise always put him in the mood for food.

"Time for something sweet," Pooh happily declared.

Pooh opened his cupboard for a pot of honey.
"Oh, bother!" Pooh cried. "Empty again.
Only the sticky part's left."
Then Pooh heard a buzzing noise. Buzzing
meant bees, and bees made honey.

"And the only reason for making honey
is so I can eat it!" Pooh decided.
Pooh followed the bee outside.

The bee flew
high up into a tree,
a tree filled with
sweet, delicious
honey.

With his tummy
rumbling, Pooh eagerly
climbed the honey tree.
He climbed, and he
climbed, and he climbed.

"Honey!" Pooh declared, reaching the top.

But the bees did not want to share with the bear.

They swarmed around Pooh until... *oh, bother!* He fell! He fell-*oof!*- and fell-*umph!*- bouncing off tree limbs until...

…he landed-*whump!*-right in the middle of a gorse bush!

"Oh, bother!" Pooh cried. "I suppose it all comes from liking honey too much!"

Pooh was even hungrier than before. What was he to do?

"Think, think, think," Pooh thought.

Pooh was joined by Christopher Robin.
Pooh saw his friend's balloon and got an idea.

"May I borrow your balloon to get honey?"
Pooh asked.

"But you don't get honey with a balloon,"
Christopher Robin answered.

"I do," Pooh said, smiling.

Then Pooh rolled in a mud puddle...

…and took the balloon from Christopher Robin.

"I shall fly up into the honey-bee tree!" Pooh explained.

"But you're not a bee," said Christopher Robin.

"They'll think I'm a little black rain cloud," Pooh answered as he rose higher and higher.

"Silly old bear!" laughed Christopher Robin. "Good luck!"

"Hello, bees!" Pooh said, reaching the top.
He tried his best to look like a little black rain
cloud, but the bees knew better. They angrily
swarmed around him.

"Christopher Robin!" Pooh called down.
"I think the bees suspect something!"

Then the balloon lost air.
It zoomed away and
took Pooh with it!

"Oh, my! Oh, help!" Pooh cried. "Christopher
Robin! I think I shall come down now."
"Don't worry, Pooh! I'll catch you."

"...*oof!*"

Pooh landed right on top of Christopher Robin!

"I have come to a very important decision," said the bear of little brain. "I do not look like a little black rain cloud."

But Pooh did not give up. He set his mind on honey. And honey rhymed with bunny, and bunny meant Rabbit.

"Hello, Rabbit," Pooh said at his friend's house. "It's lunchtime, you know."

"Oh, ah…hello, Pooh. So it is," Rabbit stammered. "Ah, join me?"

"Oh, yes!" Pooh answered. "I'd love to."

So Pooh joined Rabbit for lunch.
"Would you like milk or honey with your bread?" Rabbit grumpily asked.
"Both," Pooh replied. "But never mind the bread and never mind the milk, please."

So Pooh ate, and he ate, and he ate, and
he ate, and he ate, and he ate, and he ate,
and he ate.

"Ah, would you like some more?" Rabbit
asked, trying to sound polite.

"*Is* there any more?" Pooh asked in
a sticky voice.

"No," Rabbit replied crankily. "There isn't."

"Then I must be going," Pooh said.
"Good-bye Rabbit."

Pooh started out the door. He tried
wriggling forward. He couldn't. So he
tried wriggling backward, but he
couldn't do that either.

"Oh, help and bother!" Pooh declared.
"I'm stuck!"

It was true. Pooh's tummy was too honey-full to fit!

"Oh, dear! Oh, my! Oh, gracious!" Rabbit cried.

"It all comes from liking honey too much," Pooh sighed.

"It all comes from *eating* honey too much!" Rabbit scolded.

Rabbit pushed and pulled and shoved
and tugged. But Pooh didn't budge.

"It's no use," Rabbit cried. "I'll go get
Christopher Robin."

Poor Pooh! He tried and tried to squeeze through. He even tried to blow out air like Christopher Robin's balloon. But it didn't help. He was jammed tight.

"Well, if it isn't Pooh bear," said a familiar voice.

"Oh, hello, Owl," Pooh greeted his friend.

"You, sir, are a wedged bear in a great tightness," Owl said.

"Huh?" Pooh asked.

"You're stuck," Owl simply explained.

"This situation calls for an expert," Owl declared.

"Did someone call for an expert?" said a little newcomer. "Gopher's my name. Digging's my game."

"It seems," Owl said, "the entrance to Rabbit's domicile is impassable."

"Huh?" Gopher asked.

Rabbite Howse

"The bear's stuck," Owl explained. "What do you suggest?"

"Dynamite," Gopher replied.

"Dynamite?!" Pooh cried. "Oh, my!"

Just then Rabbit returned with Christopher Robin.

"Cheer up, Pooh," Christopher Robin said. "We'll get you out."

Rabbit
Howse

"Here, give me your arm,"
Christopher Robin said.
With Rabbit's help, Christopher Robin
grabbed and dragged and pressed and
pushed. But Pooh didn't move.

"There's only one thing we can do, Pooh,"
Christopher Robin decided. "We'll have to wait
for you to get thin again."

"How long will that take?" Pooh asked.

"Who knows?" Owl answered.

Rabbit did not want to look at Pooh's
pudgy posterior every day. But what could he do?

"If I have to face that thing," Rabbit declared,
"I might as well make the best of it."

So Rabbit decided to decorate it. First he
added a frame.

"Very nice," Rabbit said. "Now for a splash of color."
Then he placed antler-looking sticks on it and
drew a moose face.

"Not bad," Rabbit said, admiring his work. "It's
rather good, I think."

"Oh, Rabbit," Pooh called from outside.
"I have a tickle in my nose. I think I'm
going to… to…
…*ah-choo!*"
Pooh sneezed and messed up the moose!

"Why, oh, why did I
ever invite that bear
to lunch?"
moaned Rabbit.

Day after day and night after night,
everybody waited for Pooh to get thin.
The friends tried to cheer him up.
  Christopher Robin read stories to Pooh.
  Owl taught him long words.

Kanga and Roo brought Pooh a bright
blue scarf to keep him warm.

Even gloomy Eeyore tried to make
Pooh feel better.

"Well, it's better than dynamite,"
Eeyore droned.

Rabbite
Howse

One night, Gopher joined Pooh for a midnight snack.

"Ah, what sort of lunch is in that lunch box?" asked the very hungry bear.

"Oh, a pear, a squash, and some honey," Gopher answered.

"*Honey?!*" Pooh hungrily asked. "Could you spare a small smackerel?"

Rabbite Howse

DO NOT
FEED THE
BEAR

"No, no, no, no!" Rabbit cried, running out of his house. "Not one drop!"

"But, Rabbit," Pooh moaned, "I wasn't going to eat it, I was just going to taste it."

If Pooh didn't get smaller, he would never get out. So Rabbit put up a sign that read, "DO NOT FEED THE BEAR."

Then one day, just when Rabbit thought he'd never use his door again, it happened.

"He budged!" Rabbit said, pushing up against Pooh. "Hooray! Today is the day!"

Rabbit ran off to get Christopher Robin and the others.

"Everybody pull!" Christopher Robin yelled.
"Heave… ho! Heave… ho! Heave… ho!"
Slowly, slowly, slowly, Pooh started to move.
But it was too slow for Rabbit.

Rabbit stood way back from Pooh… built up
all his strength… then as fast as he could…
ran straight for the bear's backend!

Pop!
Pooh shot out of the hole!
Like a big bear-bird, Pooh soared
through the air and…

...whump!
Right into the honey tree!
The bees were terrified
and flew away.

"Don't worry, Pooh," Christopher Robin
called from the ground. "We'll get you out!"
"No hurry," Pooh replied as he grabbed
heaping handfuls of heavenly honey.
"Take your time. Take your time!"

Rabbits
Howse

Piglet

Nise For Piknics

Sandpit
where Roo playe

Owl

R SANDER☐

Pooh Bears Howse →

Floody Place

100 Aker Wood